THE KNIGHTS' TALES

THE ADVENTURES OF

Sir Lancelot the Great

GERALD MORRIS

ILLUSTRATED BY

AARON RENIER

HOUGHTON MIFFLIN COMPANY
BOSTON 2008

www.houghtonmifflinbooks.com

The text of this book is set in Post Mediaeval.
The illustrations are brush and ink.

Library of Congress Cataloging-in-Publication Data
Morris, Gerald, 1963-
The Adventures of Sir Lancelot the Great / written by Gerald Morris.
p. cm.
Summary: Relates tales of Sir Lancelot, the bravest knight in King Arthur's court.
ISBN-13: 978-0-618-77714-3
1. Lancelot (Legendary character)—Legends. 2. Arthurian romances—Adaptations. [1.
Lancelot (Legendary character)—Legends. 2. Knights and knighthood—Folklore.
3. Folklore—England.] I. Title.
PZ8.1.M8268Ad 2008
[398.20942'02]—dc22
2007041167

Manufactured in the United States of America
MP 10 9 8 7 6 5 4 3 2 1

FOR STEPHEN AND KATHERINE

CHAPTER 1

The Knight in Shining Armor

Many years ago, the storytellers say, a great king brought justice to England. The king's name was Arthur, and he surrounded himself with brave knights in shining armor, whom he sent out to defend the helpless and protect the weak. They rescued damsels in distress, slew troublesome dragons, and fought against wicked knights who used their weapons to oppress the defenseless. The wicked knights were called "recreants"—

which means something like "cowardly bullies"—and one by one they were driven from England. In this way, King Arthur brought peace to the land, and tales of his court at Camelot were told wherever people met.

Indeed, tales of King Arthur and his knights in shining armor were even told across the sea, in France, where they came to the ears of a young prince named Sir Lancelot. Sir Lancelot had just been knighted by his father, King Ban of Benouic, and although he was very young, he showed great promise in the knightly arts. When Sir Lancelot heard about King Arthur's knights, nothing would satisfy him but to join their number.

"I must go to England, to King Arthur," Sir Lancelot told King Ban, "for his knights are the greatest knights of all!"

"Are they?" asked King Ban.

"Yes, Father. They have the bravest hearts, the

noblest souls, and the shiniest armor in all the world."

"Shiniest armor?" repeated King Ban.

"Everyone says so," Sir Lancelot assured his father. "I wish to go to Camelot!"

Ban was a wise king, and an even wiser father, so he replied, "Very well. Go to Camelot. You should do well there, for you already have a brave heart and a noble soul, besides being very skilled with your weapons. You have my blessing."

"Thank you, Father," Sir Lancelot replied gratefully. "But . . . er . . . Father?"

"Yes, Lancelot?"

"You didn't say anything about my armor. Is it not shiny enough?"

A few days later, Sir Lancelot led his great horse onto a ship bound for England. He carried a long lance in one hand, and his mind was alive with dreams of glory. Arriving in England, he set out at once for Camelot, stopping only to practice with his sword and lance, to polish his armor, and to take short naps after lunch. Strictly speaking, afternoon naps were not required for knights, but Sir Lancelot found them refreshing.

On his third day, just as he began to think he should be nearing Camelot, a heavy spring rain set in. Rain is never enjoyable for someone in armor. It makes a deafening noise on the metal helmet and always leaks in at the neck and shoulders. To Sir Lancelot, though, this rain was even more distressing, because it turned the paths to mud, and in no time his armor was splashed all over with dirty spots.

When at last the rain stopped, Sir Lancelot turned his attention to his spattered appearance. Moving his lance to his left arm, he drew a towel from his saddlebags and began scrubbing at his

armored legs. Soon he was absorbed in the task, paying no attention to where his horse was taking him.

Just then, the loud drumming of a horse's hooves disturbed him from his polishing. Sir Lancelot looked up to see a knight in armor bearing down on him with his spear leveled. Realizing that this must be one of those recreant knights he'd heard of, Sir Lancelot readied himself for battle. He had no time to shift his lance to his right arm, so he met the knight's charge left-handed, popping his attacker very neatly from his saddle.

"There, now," Sir Lancelot said to the fallen knight. "Stop being so recreant and attacking people when they're busy." With that, he turned back to his armor.

A moment later, though, Sir Lancelot was interrupted again, by a different charging knight. "Bother," said Sir Lancelot, knocking the second knight from his horse. "Please go away. Can't you see I'm occupied?"

When a third knight charged just a few seconds later, Sir Lancelot began to feel annoyed. He was only halfway done with one leg, and at this rate would never get himself cleaned up. "Serves you right," he said to the third challenger after unhorsing him like the others. "You were very rude, you know."

In all, Sir Lancelot defeated sixteen knights, and was glad that English recreant knights attacked one at a time. If they had charged all at once instead of taking turns, he probably would have had to put down his towel. As it was, in between knights he was able to wipe the mud from one leg and half his breastplate.

After the parade of knights had ceased, though, a new sound disturbed Sir Lancelot's labors. Looking up, Sir Lancelot was astonished to see that he was surrounded by a crowd of people, all cheering wildly. As he stared, a smiling man in a long red cape walked up to where Sir Lancelot sat. "My goodness," said Sir Lancelot. "Where did all of you come from?"

"Unknown knight, I congratulate you!" the smiling man said. "Never have I seen such skill. You have won our tournament!"

"Tournament?" repeated Sir Lancelot blankly. "Oh! So that's why those fellows kept attacking me. They weren't recreant knights at all."

"You didn't know you were in a tournament?" the smiling man asked.

"I wasn't paying very close attention," explained Sir Lancelot. "I was busy, you see."

The man smiled more broadly. "You overcame my greatest knights without paying attention? Please, tell me your name, Sir Knight!"

"I am Sir Lancelot, just come to this land from France."

"I am delighted to meet you," the man said. "You know, I thought you must be from another land. There aren't very many left-handed knights, and I thought I knew—"

"Oh, I'm not left-handed," said Sir Lancelot.

The man's eyes widened. "But you used your left hand to unhorse all those knights!"

"My right hand was busy."

"Sir Lancelot," the man said earnestly, "I beg you to join my court, for I have never seen such skill as yours!"

"That is most kind of you, sir," replied Sir Lancelot, "but I'm afraid I cannot accept your generous offer." The man looked so disappointed that Sir Lancelot added, "Please don't be sad. It's just that I've come all this way to join King Arthur's court."

At that, the man began to laugh. "But I *am* King Arthur!"

Sir Lancelot stared for a moment, then cried out, "Oh, no! But this is awful!"

"Awful? But why?"

Sir Lancelot gestured at himself. "Look at me! I'm covered with mud! And I *did* want to make a favorable first impression!"

CHAPTER 2

The Fastest Knight in England

In no time at all, the storytellers say, Sir Lancelot became the most famous of all King Arthur's knights in shining armor. No other knight rescued so many damsels in distress or slew so many dragons or overcame so many recreant knights or, for that matter, kept his armor so tidy. He performed so many great deeds that he soon became known as Sir Lancelot the Great. Minstrels sang songs of his adventures, damsels sighed when he passed by, boys playing knights all wanted to be Sir Lancelot, and young knights dreamed of one day defeating Sir Lancelot, because whoever did that, they thought, would take his place as the greatest knight in England.

That last part soon got to be a problem. Everywhere Sir Lancelot went, knights were waiting to challenge him, all hoping to win fame and glory with one battle. Sir Lancelot defeated them all, but fighting every knight he met grew rather tiresome. So, when he rode out on a quest, he chose lonely paths. This was why he was riding alone through a quiet forest one day when he heard an unexpected sound.

"WAAAAAH!"

It was a damsel in distress. When you ride out on enough quests, you get to know that sound. Sir Lancelot turned toward the wailing and soon came to a woman sitting alone beneath a great oak tree, crying with gusto.

"Good day, my lady," Sir Lancelot said politely. It was hard to know the right thing to say at times like this.

"WAAAAAH!" the lady said.

Sir Lancelot said, "May I be of service, my lady?"

"WOOOO-HOOOO-WAAH!"

"Can you tell me what is distressing you, my lady?"

"WAAAH! BLUH-BLUH-WOO-WAAH!"

"I'll just wait here a bit, then, shall I?"

"WIBBLE-BLIDDER-WO-WO-HAH-WAAH!"

So Sir Lancelot sat on his horse and waited. No one can cry forever, and when at last the lady had used up all her tears, Sir Lancelot asked again, "Can you tell me what is distressing you?"

"It's my . . . my fal-fal-falcon!" the lady gasped.

Now in those days, noble lords and ladies used

to train falcons to hunt for them. They kept them on leashes, then set them free to hunt small birds. A well-trained falcon—that is, one that would come back—was quite valuable.

"What happened to your falcon, my lady?"

"It flew away! It was a gift from my husband," the woman wailed, beginning to cry again. Not all falcons were well trained.

"I'm sorry to hear it, my lady," said Sir Lancelot. "I wish I could help you."

"Would you?" the woman exclaimed, her tears stopping at once.

"Er . . . if I could," Sir Lancelot replied. "But how? I can't chase a falcon through the sky."

"Oh, you don't have to chase her at all," the woman said, smiling brightly. "She's right up there!" The woman pointed up. There at the top of the oak tree was a falcon, her leash tangled in the small branches.

"Oh," said Sir Lancelot.

"You said you'd help," the woman reminded him.

"Er . . . yes, I did. The thing is, it's rather hard to climb trees in armor."

"Can't you take your armor off?" the woman asked. She sniffled.

Sir Lancelot frowned. He had just had his armor shined and didn't like to leave it lying around. Then he sighed. "Of course, my lady."

Twenty minutes later, his armor and sword stacked neatly beside a bush, Sir Lancelot began climbing the tree. While he climbed, he wondered how to untangle an angry falcon from a tree without getting pecked, but soon he saw what to do. Coming to the branch where the bird was tangled, he simply broke it off at the base and tossed the whole branch free. Bird and branch fluttered and crashed to the ground, and Sir Lancelot wiped his brow with relief.

"Ha-ha, Sir Lancelot the Great!" shouted a gruff voice. Sir Lancelot looked down. Things had changed below. The crying woman was gone, and in her place stood an armored knight with a drawn sword. "Pretty neat, hey?" the knight crowed.

"I beg your pardon?" Sir Lancelot replied.

"I got you to take off your armor and put away your sword! Now you're helpless, and when I've slain you, I, Sir Phelot, will be known as the greatest knight in England!"

"Sir Phelot?"

"That's right," the knight replied. "Sir Phelot the Great."

"Pleased to meet you," Sir Lancelot murmured. "So all this business with the falcon was a trick?"

"That's right," Sir Phelot said. "Clever, hey?"

"And that lady was your wife?"

"Don't be silly. She's an actress. I've already paid her and sent her off."

"An actress?" repeated Sir Lancelot admiringly. "She's very good, isn't she?"

"Yes, yes," Sir Phelot said curtly. "And now I have you! Come down from that tree and face your doom!"

Sir Lancelot looked at Sir Phelot for a long moment, then stretched out on a sturdy branch. "No," he said.

"What do you mean, 'no'?" Sir Phelot demanded.

"I'm comfortable," said Sir Lancelot. He leaned against the trunk of the tree and closed his eyes.

"Oh, for heaven's sake," Sir Phelot said. "Whatever do you think you're doing? You can't stay up in that tree forever!"

"Why not?"

"Well, you'll get hungry, for one thing," Sir Phelot said.

"So will you," Sir Lancelot pointed out.

Sir Phelot frowned over this for a moment. If he left the tree to get food, Sir Lancelot would get away. "Well . . . you have to sleep sometime."

Sir Lancelot only smiled.

"Oh, stop being so childish!" snapped Sir Phelot, stamping his foot. "You know perfectly well that you have to come down eventually."

Sir Lancelot ignored him. Licking his lips, he began to whistle softly, trying to remember a song that he had heard from a minstrel at King Arthur's court.

"What's that noise?" Sir Phelot demanded.

"It's a love song," Sir Lancelot replied. "It's called 'Llude Sing Cuckoo.'"

"*What* sing cuckoo?"

"'Llude,'" Sir Lancelot said. "I think it means loud."

"Why not say so, then?"

Sir Lancelot sniffed. "You obviously don't understand art. Actually, this is quite a lucky chance for me. Back at court when I sing, people always remember that they have somewhere else to be. Sir Gawain says that I'm tone deaf, but he's Scottish and listens to bagpipes, so how would he know?" With that, Sir Lancelot burst into enthusiastic song.

> *"Summer is i-cumin in!*
> *Llude sing cuckoo!"*

Sir Phelot removed his helmet and covered his ears, so Sir Lancelot sang it again, louder this time. He sang for more than an hour, until his voice grew tired. He didn't know any other songs. In fact, he only knew those two lines of this one, but he didn't mind singing the same lines over and over. Sir Phelot stuffed wadded-up leaves in his ears and covered his head with his arms, but he was still making whimpering noises by the time Sir Lancelot's voice grew weary.

No one can sing forever, though, and at last Sir Lancelot stopped. Sir Phelot carefully removed his earplugs and peeked up the tree. "Are you done?" he asked.

Sir Lancelot didn't reply. He was looking at a cluster of acorns not far from his head. Picking one acorn, he held it out over Sir Phelot and let it drop.

Plink! went the acorn off Sir Phelot's armor.

"Stop that!" Sir Phelot said.

Plink! Plink! Thonk!

"That one sounded different," Sir Lancelot said. "What did it hit?"

Sir Phelot put his helmet back on.

Plink!

"WILL YOU KINDLY CUT THAT OUT!" shouted Sir Phelot. He began jumping up and down and waving his arms and growling fiercely. He scuffed the dirt with his feet, then kicked the base of the tree very hard. Then he said a great many colorful words and sat down, holding his foot with one hand and screaming with frustration. Sir Lancelot stopped throwing acorns and watched Sir Phelot's tantrum with interest. Sir Phelot cursed and roared and threatened and screamed for a very long time, but at last he grew hoarse and lapsed into panting silence.

Plink!

Sir Lancelot thought he heard a sobbing noise from inside Sir Phelot's helmet, but then Sir Phelot leaped to his feet. "No! I won't give up! I *will* defeat Sir Lancelot and become the greatest knight in England!"

Plink!

"You're just making it worse for yourself, you know! You're making me angry!"

Plinkety-plinkety-plink-plink-plink!

"STOP THAT! If you don't stop dropping nuts on me I'll . . . I'll . . . I'll just cut down your tree!"

Sir Lancelot stopped throwing acorns and said admiringly, "Now, that's quite clever. You should go home and get an ax at once!"

Sir Phelot laughed. "How stupid do you think I am?"

Sir Lancelot did not reply.

"I'm going to cut down the tree with my sword!" Sir Phelot declared.

"Ah!" Sir Lancelot said, very softly. "*That* stupid." He dropped two more acorns.

Plink! Plink!

With a roar of rage, Sir Phelot drew back his sword and swung it with all his strength against the trunk of the tree. The blade sank deep into the wood. Sir Phelot chuckled to himself, then tugged the hilt sharply.

The sword remained in the tree. Sir Phelot tugged it again, harder. He walked around the tree and kicked it. He braced one foot, then both feet, against the trunk and pulled with all his might. The blade wouldn't budge.

While he tugged and yanked and grunted over his sword, Sir Lancelot quietly climbed down the tree and dropped noiselessly to the ground. Taking up his own sword, he stepped behind Sir Phelot.

"Do you need some help?"

"No, thank you," Sir Phelot snapped irritably. "I can do it myself."

"What if you tried to pry it out with another sword?"

Sir Phelot turned around and snapped, "Now where am I going to find another ... er ... another ... oh, dear."

It is very difficult to run fast or far while wearing armor, but the storytellers say that that day Sir Phelot broke all the records. In fact, the run of Sir Phelot became proverbial in King Arthur's court. Sir Phelot was called "the fastest knight in England" and every exceptionally speedy runner would be called a "regular Sir Phelot." And so, as it happened, Sir Phelot did become famous for his speed, and perhaps that would have satisfied him. No one can say for sure, though, because Sir Phelot was never seen in England again.

CHAPTER 3
Sir Kay's Restful Quest

Although Sir Lancelot usually rode alone when he went questing, one time he agreed to ride with a friend, Sir Kay. Sir Kay was King Arthur's foster brother, and years before had been one of the heroes of Camelot. But Sir Kay was older now and seldom went out questing these days, so when he did, he thought it would be good to have Sir Lancelot along. After all, he thought, who would dare challenge the greatest knight in England? Sir Kay looked forward to a restful quest.

After three days, though, Sir Kay wasn't sure. They met no dragons to slay, no recreant knights, and not one damsel in even a tiny bit of distress. "Restful" began to feel a lot like "boring." Worst of all, to Sir Kay's astonishment, every afternoon Sir Lancelot stopped for a nap.

"Naps?" expostulated Sir Kay. "Is this what you call questing?"

"I like afternoon naps," Sir Lancelot explained. "They're very refreshing."

So for three days, after lunch, Sir Kay sat around while his companion refreshed himself. "This is taking restfulness too far," Sir Kay muttered on the third afternoon. "I suppose I could look about for a *little* adventure while Lancelot has his beauty sleep." With that, Sir Kay mounted his horse and cantered off into the forest.

When Sir Lancelot awoke that day, he knew at once that something was wrong. To begin with, he had been awakened by someone tightening ropes around his hands and feet, which was not at all normal. Also, at his feet sat four ladies in crowns, and he couldn't remember ever waking up with queens at his feet. Sir Kay was nowhere to be seen.

"Er, good afternoon, Your Highnesses," said Sir Lancelot.

"You're Sir Lancelot, aren't you?" one queen asked breathlessly.

"Yes, I am. Why are my hands—?"

All four queens squealed with delight. "I knew it!" the first queen said.

"I recognized his shining armor," said the second.

"I knew it from his shield," said the third.

"He's *so* handsome!" added the fourth.

"Is it true you've never lost a tournament?" asked the first.

"Did you really defeat the great Sir Carados?" added the second.

"And slay the two giants of Tintagel?" queried the third.

"He's *so* handsome!" said the fourth.

"My ladies," replied Sir Lancelot. "May I ask your names?"

The first lady replied, "I am the Queen of Gor. This is the Queen of Northgales, the Queen of Eastland, and the Queen of the Out Isles."

"He's *so* handsome!" commented the Queen of the Out Isles.

"Charmed to meet you," Sir Lancelot said. "And, if I may ask, why are my hands and feet tied?"

"It's only temporary," the Queen of Gor assured him. "We've sent for soldiers from my castle, and as soon as they put you in my dungeon, we can remove your bonds."

"Your dungeon?"

"Just for a little while," the Queen of Gor said, smiling. "You'll be freed soon."

"How soon?" asked Sir Lancelot.

"As soon as you choose one of us for your true love."

"Do choose me!" interjected the Queen of Northgales.

"No, pick me!" cried the Queen of Eastland.

"He's *so* handsome!" added the Queen of the Out Isles.

"Ah," said Sir Lancelot wearily. "*That* soon."

For two days Sir Lancelot paced back and forth in the Queen of Gor's dungeon. Every morning, the queens trooped in and asked him to choose one of them as his love forever, and every morning, Sir Lancelot politely declined. The only other person he saw was the Queen of Gor's lady-in-waiting, Blanche, who fed him.

"How are you today?" asked Blanche as she brought him lunch on the second day.

"Since you ask," replied Sir Lancelot, "not very well."

"Have you chosen one of the queens to love yet?" asked Blanche.

"The thing is," Sir Lancelot explained, "I *don't* love one of them. At the moment, in fact, I don't even like them."

"To be honest," Blanche said, "they're getting annoyed with you, too. Except the Queen of the Out Isles, of course. She thinks—"

"I know," sighed Sir Lancelot. "I'm *so* handsome."

"Well, yes, she does rather think that," Blanche admitted. She hesitated briefly, then said, "Sir Lancelot?"

"Yes?"

"If I accidentally left your door unlocked, would you escape and find your way out of the castle, remembering to go left at every turning?"

Sir Lancelot blinked. "I might," he admitted. "Left at every turn, you say?"

"That's right. And if you did find your way out and recover your horse and armor from the stables—the last stall on the right—would you go looking for adventure?"

"Perhaps," said Sir Lancelot.

"And if you went seeking adventure and found a strong recreant knight named Sir Turquin the Rotten, who locks up all the knights he defeats in his dungeons, would you fight him and make him set his prisoners free, including a knight named Sir Bademus, who happens to be my brother?"

"I would do my best, my lady," replied Sir Lancelot.

"Oh," said Blanche. "I just wondered." Then she left, without locking the door.

Following Blanche's directions, Sir Lancelot escaped from the dungeon, recovered his horse and armor, and rode away from the Castle of Gor. He had two tasks before him: first, to face this Sir Turquin, and second, to find Sir Kay. As fortune would have it, he completed both tasks at once.

Riding through a wood shortly after his escape, Sir Lancelot heard a muffled groan, then the slow clopping of hooves. A moment later he came upon Sir Kay, bound and slung face-down over his saddle, while a knight in black armor led Sir Kay's horse.

"Kay?" said Sir Lancelot.

Sir Kay twisted around and, with effort, looked up at him. "Where the deuce have you been?"

"It's a long story," replied Sir Lancelot. "Er, how've you been?"

"Actually," said Sir Kay, "not so well. I don't suppose you could lend a hand, could you?"

Sir Lancelot turned toward the black knight, who demanded gruffly, "Are you a friend of Sir Kay's?"

"I am."

"Then know this! I am Sir Turquin the Rotten, and I hate all knights but especially those of King Arthur's court! I have sworn to attack all such knights that I meet!"

"Why?" asked Sir Lancelot.

Sir Turquin scowled. "Because I'm a recreant knight, of course! It's what we do!"

"I see," replied Sir Lancelot. "Just following the rules, then?"

"Somebody has to," said Sir Turquin. "If only to keep the tradition alive. If you saw the shoddy work some of the young recreant knights are doing these days, you'd be shocked!"

"Excuse me," interrupted Sir Kay. "If you two are quite done chatting . . ."

"Oh, right," Sir Lancelot said apologetically. He and Sir Turquin drew their swords and charged each other.

It was a magnificent battle, if you like that sort of thing. Sir Lancelot had fought many great knights, but never had he faced so skillful a swordsman. They traded blows for more than an hour, which is quite a long time to fight in full armor. At last, exhausted, the two knights separated for a moment, gasping for breath.

"I had . . . had no idea . . . recreant knights . . . could do such good work," panted Sir Lancelot.

"Thanks," gasped Sir Turquin. "I do . . . take pride in my . . . my craft. You're . . . you're rather good, yourself."

"You're too kind," Sir Lancelot replied modestly.

Sir Turquin took a deep breath. "It goes against . . . against the grain to put such a fine knight in my dungeon. I'd like to propose a truce. Unless, of course . . ." he trailed off.

"Unless what?"

"There's one knight I cannot have a truce with,"

said Sir Turquin. "The knight who defeated my brother, Sir Carados. I have sworn never to make peace with Sir Lancelot."

Sir Lancelot sighed. "What a shame!" he said.

"Oh," replied Sir Turquin. "I see."

With that, the two knights raised their weapons and hurled themselves at each other again, for another hour. Sir Kay, hanging upside down, saw little of the battle, of course, but from what he saw, he always said afterward that never had such a fight been waged in England. As for Sir Lancelot, he would only say that that he did not so much defeat Sir Turquin as outlast him.

But outlast him he did. After the second hour, Sir Lancelot managed to land one blow on Sir Turquin's helmet that stunned the black knight for a moment. Another blow, and Sir Turquin sank to his knees, then toppled over on his face, unconscious. Staggering and barely conscious himself,

Sir Lancelot untied his friend. Then Sir Kay helped the exhausted Sir Lancelot onto his horse and led the way to Sir Turquin's castle. An hour later, the two friends were being joyfully thanked by dozens of knights whom they had released from Sir Turquin's dungeons. Among the freed knights were many friends from Camelot, as well as Sir Bademus, Blanche's brother.

"Let's go find a quiet place in the woods, Kay," Sir Lancelot said. "I need my afternoon nap. If you don't mind, would you wake me up tomorrow afternoon?"

CHAPTER 4
Return and Departure

After their encounter with Sir Turquin, Sir Lancelot and Sir Kay rested for several days, until both felt strong enough to ride. At last, Sir Lancelot announced that he felt fit enough to face adventures again.

"Er, haven't we just faced one?" Sir Kay asked, surprised.

"Yes," Sir Lancelot replied, "but I'm sure there are others."

Sir Kay thought about this for a moment. "Don't you think we should leave some adventures for Arthur's other knights? We don't want to be piggy, you know."

"I never thought of that," admitted Sir Lancelot.

"Besides that," added Sir Kay, "I don't heal from knocks as quickly as I used to. I'd as soon not do any more fighting for a bit. To be honest, I'm ready to go home."

"I understand perfectly," Sir Lancelot said. "But I'm feeling fine, and it seems a shame not to find at least one more adventure while I'm out. Just one more wouldn't be greedy, would it?"

"Tell you what," Sir Kay said. "Why don't we split up? I'll go back to court and report on our quest together, and you can shop around for another adventure. And I've had another idea, too. Why don't we exchange armor?"

"What?"

"I'll wear your armor and you'll wear mine,"

Sir Kay explained.

"Why?"

"Everyone knows your shining armor, don't you see? When recreant knights see me, they'll think that I'm you and leave me alone. Who would want to fight Sir Lancelot the Great?"

"Sir Turquin did," Sir Lancelot pointed out.

"And look how that turned out for him," Sir Kay replied. "No, I'm sure it will give me a quiet, restful ride home."

"But Kay," Sir Lancelot began, "when people see my armor, they usually—"

"Meanwhile," Sir Kay continued, "you'll be in my armor, which nobody knows. It will be like a disguise, and you'll have all sorts of adventures you wouldn't have had otherwise. What do you say?"

Sir Lancelot tried to argue, but his friend persisted, and in the end he agreed. Over the next few weeks, it did seem that Sir Kay had been right. Although he missed his own armor, Sir

Lancelot had a great many adventures, and England's storytellers began to tell how Sir Kay overcame a recreant knight named Sir Peris of the Forest Savage and how how he drove away an evil sorceress named Hellawes of the Chapel Perilous, and many other such stories. At last, Sir Lancelot returned to court, where the first knight to meet him was Sir Kay.

"Thank goodness you're home!" Sir Kay declared.

"Oh? Did you miss me?" asked Sir Lancelot.

"Deuced right, I did!" Sir Kay exclaimed. "Now give me my armor and take yours back at once!"

Sir Lancelot smiled. "Didn't you like my shining armor?"

"Not by half! You might have warned me that everywhere I went, every wet-eared, knock-kneed thimblewit who fancies himself a knight would try to fight me!"

"That does get inconvenient, doesn't it? But truly, I tried to warn you."

"But those silly puppies weren't the worst of it!" continued Sir Kay. "Not ten miles from where we parted, I was set on by four of the nastiest wenches I've ever met—all of them wearing crowns—crying and wailing and snatching at my feet and throwing themselves on me and calling out, 'Choose me, Sir Lancelot!' and 'Come back, Sir Lancelot!' and 'You're *so* handsome, Sir Lancelot!'"

"Oh, you met the four queens. Perhaps I should have mentioned them to you."

"I should dashed well think so! I was lucky to get away in one piece!" Sir Kay threw Sir Lancelot's armor down between them. "I'll tell you this, Lancelot. I used to envy you, but now that I've tried it, I wouldn't be in your place for anything!"

Sir Lancelot sighed. Sir Kay had a point: being Sir Lancelot the Great was not very restful.

The very next day Sir Lancelot learned that being the greatest knight in England had other disadvantages. As it happened, a few days before Sir Lancelot arrived at court, King Arthur had proclaimed a tournament, to the delight of all Camelot. There would be jousting, which was where knights tried to knock one another from their horses with lances, and a mock battle and colorful banners and minstrels and jugglers and feasts. All the brave knights polished their armor, and all the fair damsels gave tokens to their favorite knights, bright strips of cloth to wear on their armor. The event was scheduled for two weeks away, and all Camelot buzzed with anticipation.

Sir Lancelot was delighted as well. He always enjoyed a good tournament, and so he declared that he would enter the contest.

"Oh, well," said all the brave knights, putting away their armor.

"Never mind," said all the fair damsels, taking back their tokens.

"Lancelot," said King Arthur, "I wonder if I could ask you to give this tournament a miss?"

"But why, Sire?" asked Sir Lancelot.

"The thing is," the king replied, "all the other knights know that you'll win, and all the damsels know that you never wear a lady's token in a joust. It just takes the fun out of it for the everyone else."

"But I *like* tournaments," Sir Lancelot said. "What if I promise to use my left hand?"

"You've already defeated everyone left-handed,"

King Arthur pointed out. "I'm afraid you'll need a bigger handicap than that to make it fair. Tell you what, Lance, why don't you take a little vacation in the countryside?"

"I've just come back from the countryside."

"Then find a *different* countryside."

"Bother," Sir Lancelot said, but he obeyed and left the court.

As the king had suggested, Sir Lancelot rode to a countryside he had never visited before, a pleasant region called Shalott. Around midafternoon, Sir Lancelot found a shady spot under a tree and, after removing his armor, lay down for his afternoon nap.

Hardly had he gone to sleep, though, when he was roused by the baying of hunting dogs nearby, then the murmur of human voices. He was about to sit up to look about when he was struck with a searing pain in the part of his body that he normally sat upon. On the right side. Sir Lancelot gasped but stayed still, listening. Someone, it seemed, was attacking him, and he wanted to know who.

Behind him, a woman's voice said, "Did I hit it?"

"No, you didn't hit it," replied a man's voice. "I *told* you to get closer before shooting."

"But it was a very *big* deer. I thought I couldn't miss."

"Elaine, you duffer, you couldn't have hit a deer at that distance if it had been as big as a house. Even *I* wouldn't have tried that shot!"

"Ooh," retorted the woman. "Even the great Sir Lavaine wouldn't have tried it!"

"And now you've lost a perfectly good arrow somewhere in that tall grass," the man replied.

With much discomfort, Sir Lancelot pulled himself to his feet. Across the meadow stood a young woman and a young man. "Excuse me," Sir

Lancelot said. The two looked at him with surprise. "Have you lost an arrow?" he asked them.

"Yes, indeed," the young lady replied. "Have you seen it?"

"Not exactly," said Sir Lancelot. "But I know where it is."

"See, I haven't lost it after all," the lady said to the man. She smiled at Sir Lancelot. "Would you show me where it landed?"

"Er, I'd rather not, my lady," Sir Lancelot said. His leg was wet with blood, and he was starting to feel dizzy. "Do either of you know where I could find a doctor hereabouts?"

Then Sir Lancelot fainted.

CHAPTER 5

The Lady of Shalott

When Sir Lancelot awoke he was lying on his stomach in a bed, and beside him sat two men—the young man from the meadow and an older man in rich clothes and a gray beard.

"Oh, good," the young man said. "You're awake."

"Ouch," said Sir Lancelot.

"I'm afraid you'll smart for a while," the older man said. "And be quite weak for a bit. The doctor says you've lost a lot of blood."

"Where am I?"

"I am Sir Bernard of Shalott, and you're in my castle. My daughter, Lady Elaine, and Sir Lavaine here brought you to me after you fainted."

"And where is the lady—Lady Elaine?" Sir Lancelot asked.

"We made her leave while the doctor treated your . . . um, your wound," Sir Lavaine explained.

"That was thoughtful of you," Sir Lancelot said faintly.

"She'll be back soon, though," Sir Lavaine said. "She feels awful about this. It *was* an accident, you know."

"I'm sure it was," Sir Lancelot murmured.

"I mean, it *couldn't* have been on purpose," Sir Lavaine went on. "Elaine couldn't have hit your—hit such a target at that distance for any price. To tell the truth, you'd have been safer if she *had* been aiming at you."

"That's not true!" declared a female voice from

behind Sir Lancelot. "And even if it were, it's very unhandsome of you to say so, Lavaine."

"I'm only speaking truth, Elaine. The day you learn to—"

"As if you could do better!"

"Please don't argue," interrupted Sir Lancelot wearily. "It gives me a pain in the—it makes my wound hurt."

"I know just how you feel," Lady Elaine said, walking up to the head of the bed. "Sir Lavaine has given me that same pain for years. But truly, Sir Knight, I must tell you how sorry I—oh, my!" She broke off, staring at Sir Lancelot. "Well!" she said. "Aren't you a handsome fellow! I must say, if I had to shoot a knight, at least I bagged a good one!"

"Elaine!" said Sir Lavaine reproachfully. "You don't sound sorry at all! Don't you realize what you've done? I'm sure that this knight here was on his way to the great tournament at Camelot, and now thanks to you he'll have to miss it!"

"Piffle!" Lady Elaine said with a snort. "Why should a little scratch like that keep him from a tournament?"

"Because he won't be able to ride a horse, that's why! No knight could joust with such a handicap!"

"What's that?" asked Sir Lancelot suddenly. "Did you say *handicap?*"

"I certainly did. Don't you think that a wound in the—a wound like yours would be a handicap? Why, Sir Lancelot himself couldn't win a tournament in your condition! By the way, sir. What *is* your name?"

Sir Lancelot smiled. "John. My name is Sir John," he said.

Except for having to carry a pillow everywhere with him to sit on, Sir Lancelot had a lovely vacation at the Castle of Shalott, where he was cared for attentively by Lady Elaine and enjoyed long

talks with Sir Bernard and also with the young Sir Lavaine, who lived nearby and rode over nearly every day.

After a week, just two days before the king's tournament, Sir Lancelot revealed his plan. "Sir Bernard," he asked his host. "Do you have any old armor lying about that I could borrow?"

"Whatever for?" asked Sir Bernard.

"I'd like to wear it in the tournament at Camelot."

"What? With a great, gaping wound in your—"

"I'm feeling much better, actually."

"How will you ride a horse?"

"I thought I would use a pillow."

Sir Bernard gawked at him. "A tournament knight with a pillow on his saddle? You'll look ridiculous!"

"That's why I don't want to wear my own armor," Sir Lancelot said promptly. "I'll be in disguise, so that if I end up looking silly, no one will know me."

Sir Bernard still tried to talk him out of his plan, and so did Sir Lavaine when he heard of it. "You're mad!" Sir Lavaine said. "I won't let you go!"

"How will you stop me?" Sir Lancelot asked.

"I . . . I don't know, but . . . Well, I won't let you go alone, anyway. Someone has to carry you off to a doctor when you faint. I'm coming too."

Only Lady Elaine approved of Sir Lancelot's

idea. "I *told* you it was just a little scratch, Mister Smarty-Armor," she said to Sir Lavaine. "I think Sir John will be fine. In fact, I believe it so much that I'm going to give him my sleeve to wear as a token in the tournament."

Sir Lancelot started to say that he never wore ladies' tokens, but then he realized this would give him away. The only knight who had that rule was Sir Lancelot. In fact, if he did wear Lady Elaine's token, it would add to his disguise. "I would be honored to wear your token," Sir Lancelot said graciously, but to tell the truth he wasn't happy about it.

Neither, Sir Lancelot saw too late, was Sir Lavaine.

CHAPTER 6
The Knight of the Pillow

By the time Sir Lancelot, Sir Lavaine, and Lady Elaine arrived at Camelot, Sir Lancelot was more certain than ever that he should not have accepted Lady Elaine's token. Wearing a lady's token was often seen as a mark of love, which was why Sir Lancelot never wore them—he didn't want to give a lady a false impression—and even though he didn't think Lady Elaine loved him, wearing her token might give someone the wrong idea. Sir Lavaine, for instance, had been cold and distant to him ever since he had accepted Lady Elaine's offer. He had also been rather cool toward Lady Elaine, and Sir Lancelot was saddened to think he had come between the two friends.

Once they arrived at the tournament, though, Sir Lancelot had little time to worry about such matters. The tournament was about to begin, and he and Sir Lavaine had to hurry to their places for the jousting.

When Sir Lancelot appeared for his first joust and the crowds saw the cushion tied to his saddle, they all laughed and jeered, but as the day wore on and Sir Lancelot won every contest, their laughter was replaced with cheers. The jousting wasn't easy for Sir Lancelot, of course. His wound hurt more and more as the day went on, and he found himself leaning to his left, off balance, as he rode. Several times he was nearly unhorsed, but somehow he always prevailed.

The crowd buzzed with speculation. Who was this knight? Sir Lancelot had given his name only as "The Unknown," but by the end of the first day all Camelot was talking about the "Knight of the Pillow." Lady Elaine, watching from the stands, cheered delightedly at every victory and in her excitement told the lady sitting beside her that the Knight of the Pillow was wearing her token. At once she was almost as celebrated as Sir Lancelot, which she rather enjoyed. As for Sir Lavaine, he did very well, too, though few noticed.

Having arrived together, Sir Lancelot and Sir Lavaine had been assigned to share a tent, and at the end of the first day Sir Lancelot could hardly wait to collapse, exhausted, on his cot there. He was much weaker than he had thought. Sir

Lavaine left him to rest and went out for an evening stroll, but he very soon returned, a stormy expression on his face.

"Congratulations, Sir John," he said upon entering the tent.

"On what?" asked Sir Lancelot.

"On your upcoming marriage," replied Sir Lavaine.

"My what?"

"Don't you know? It's all over the camp that you love Elaine, the Lady of Shalott, and that the two of you are to be married after the tournament."

Sir Lancelot gaped at him. "Who said such a thing?"

"*Everyone* says such a thing, Sir John. I hope you'll both be very happy."

"But Sir Lavaine," Sir Lancelot protested, "I don't really love—"

"You aren't going to break Elaine's heart, are you?" snapped Sir Lavaine angrily.

Sir Lancelot lapsed into silence. He knew how rumors could fly at court, and he was sure that this whole story had been built up from that silly token. Elaine didn't love him—he had an idea that she loved someone else—but what a muddle it all was!

"Welcome, O knights!" called out King Arthur the next morning, the final day of the tournament. This day was to be a mock battle, in which all the best knights from the first day rode into a field and fought. The rules weren't difficult: the last knight still on his horse won. "So far," King Arthur continued, "the best knight has been the Knight of the Pillow, but today we will see if he shall prove the winner!" Then the king smiled. "But if what I hear is true, then you shall be a winner either way, O knight, for I hear that after the games the knight who wears that token is to marry the beautiful Lady of Shalott."

The knights applauded, the ladies sighed, and Sir Lavaine gave a snort, but Sir Lancelot was watching Lady Elaine, whose eyes widened with dismay. Now Sir Lancelot knew he had been right; Lady Elaine had never said any such thing.

Then the contest began, and Sir Lancelot had no time to think of anything but defending himself, for of course all the other knights were trying to unhorse the one who had won the first day. Again and again he narrowly escaped attacks, but he knew it couldn't last forever. He could feel himself weakening as the battle went on, and despite his pillow, his wound hurt awfully. He knew he had been foolish to enter the tournament.

The end came at last. He was cornered at one side of the field by four knights, and he could hardly lift his weary arms. He braced himself for a blow, but just then a shout came across the field— "Hold on, Sir John! I'm coming!"—and then, with a

pounding of hooves and a ringing battle cry, Sir Lavaine charged into Sir Lancelot's attackers.

Sir Lancelot watched with respect as Sir Lavaine unhorsed two knights with his first rush, then wheeled and took on the next knight with his sword at close quarters. Sir Lavaine was fighting brilliantly, but even so, four knights were too many. He brought down the third knight but was himself unhorsed by the fourth.

Summoning his last ounce of strength, Sir Lancelot raised his lance and drove that fourth knight to the ground. Then he looked around and saw to his surprise that he was the only knight still on his horse.

"You have won, O Knight of the Pillow," announced King Arthur. All the court had gathered at the royal pavilion to watch the king award the prize, a medallion of flashing gold, to the winner.

To one side, Sir Lancelot saw Sir Lavaine and Lady Elaine standing together, whispering urgently. The king raised the medallion. "Step forward, O knight, and receive your prize."

Sir Lancelot bowed but did not move. "I cannot, your highness."

All the court, even Sir Lavaine and Lady Elaine, fell silent.

"You cannot?" repeated the king.

"No, Sire," said Sir Lancelot. "I was not the best knight here today. You all saw what happened. I was lost until another knight rescued me by defeating three knights single-handedly. Please, Sire, give the prize to Sir Lavaine."

King Arthur smiled. "As you wish, O Knight of the Pillow."

"And as for me," Sir Lancelot continued, "I will give Sir Lavaine another prize." With that, Sir Lancelot removed Lady Elaine's red token from his armor and took it to Sir Lavaine. "Now, Sir Lavaine," he said gravely, "you heard what King Arthur said this morning, that the knight who wears this token must marry the Lady of Shalott."

"Oh!" said Lady Elaine, blushing. "But, I promise you, I never said—"

"Thank you, O Knight of the Pillow," interrupted Sir Lavaine. "I should like that."

"You would?" said Elaine, her eyes shining. "Oh! Well, if I must I must."

King Arthur smiled at Sir Lancelot. "You are as gracious as you are brave, O knight. May I ask your true name?"

Sir Lancelot nodded and removed his helmet. All the court gasped, "Sir Lancelot!"

"Sir Lancelot?" whispered Lady Elaine.

"Heavens!" exclaimed Sir Lavaine. "Do you see what this means, Elaine? It means that you shot England's greatest knight in the—"

"But . . . but . . . but it was an accident!" she said. "You don't mind, do you, Sir Lancelot?"

"Of course not," Sir Lancelot replied. "It was a fine adventure. Just promise me that when I come to visit you and your children in years to come that you'll leave your bow and arrows alone."

And the Lady of Shalott promised.

CHAPTER 7
Sir Lancelot the Retired

Sir Lancelot had been thinking about his future, and the more he thought, the gloomier he felt. What he'd been thinking was that being a knight in shining armor wasn't all it was cracked up to be.

He knew that he was very good at what he did, and that he ought to be content, but he wasn't. Nothing ever seemed to turn out as it should. He had won great honor for his skill, but that had only made him a target for ambitious knights and scheming ladies. He had enjoyed winning tournaments, but his victories had only ruined the fun for everyone else. It had been pleasant to be a knight in disguise, but even that had caused problems, putting Sir Kay in danger and nearly ruining everything for Lady Elaine and Sir Lavaine. His problem, as he saw it, was that the thing that he did best was the very thing that kept making trouble for himself and his friends.

At last Sir Lancelot made his decision. Going to King Arthur, he said, "Sire, I would like to retire from the Round Table and leave Camelot."

The king stared. "Retire? Leave? But why, Lance?"

"I am not happy, my king."

"Not . . . Look here, Lance, if this is about some lady you've fallen in love with, I could talk to her and—"

"It's not that, Sire."

King Arthur sighed. "Well, I didn't *think* so. After all, it seems as if all the ladies in the court would be glad to have you, judging from the way they follow you . . . everywhere . . . Oh, I think I see."

Sir Lancelot nodded. "Yes, I would like to go where no one follows me."

The king bowed his head sadly. "You must do what seems best to you, my friend. Go in peace, Lance."

Sir Kay understood, too, when Sir Lancelot told him. "I remember saying once that I wouldn't be you for anything," he said.

"Yes," replied Sir Lancelot. "I'd like to put away my shining armor and stop being Sir Lancelot for a while."

But Sir Kay only smiled. "You can put off the armor, anyway," he said, and then Sir Lancelot left Camelot.

Sir Lancelot rode into a dense and pathless forest. Along the way, he came to a lake, and after removing his sword and shining armor, he threw them in. Two days later, he rode up to a rough cabin in a small clearing, where an old man sat on a three-legged stool. Sir Lancelot stared. "I didn't think anyone lived in this forest!" he exclaimed.

The old man smiled. "And I didn't think anyone ever passed through this forest." He rose to his feet. "But I don't mind a visitor. My name is Brastias."

Sir Lancelot nodded in greeting. "And I'm Sir . . .
er . . . I'm Lancelot."

Brastias said, "Lancelot? What an interesting
name. I don't think I've ever heard that one before."

Sir Lancelot smiled wider. "Really? How won-
derful! You've lived here long?"

"Twenty winters now, ever since I gave up being a knight."

"You used to be a knight?"

"Yes," replied Brastias. "But I didn't like it, so I
came here to the deepest forest in the land, found
a clearing, and built a cabin. I live a quiet life here,
eating what the forest provides."

Sir Lancelot sighed thoughtfully. "That sounds
nice. But what do you do all day?"

Brastias stroked his beard. "Well," he said, "I take
naps every afternoon."

Sir Lancelot's eyes gleamed. "Are there any
other clearings hereabouts?"

CHAPTER **8**
The Poisoned Pear

While Sir Lancelot made a new life for himself, trouble came to Camelot. There was one knight at Camelot who did not love King Arthur. His name was Sir Mador de la Porte. Sir Mador's brother had been a recreant knight, one whom King Arthur had banished from England, and although Sir Mador smiled and outwardly made himself agreeable, all his inward thoughts were of revenge.

Sir Mador had woven many plans, but he wanted his vengeance to be perfect. He had thought of ways to kill the king, but that was not enough for him. He didn't want the king to die; he wanted the king to suffer. Sir Mador decided to kill Queen Guinevere instead.

So it happened that about a year after Sir Lancelot retired from the Round Table, Sir Mador took action. During the bustle of preparations for a feast, he managed to slip a poisoned pear into the bowl of fruit that Queen Guinevere always kept at her place. But that night the queen was not hungry and only picked at her food. She ate so little that a young knight named Sir Patrise, once he had finished his own meal, asked if she were feeling well. The queen smiled at him and said, "I am just not hungry this evening. But don't let me slow you down, Sir Patrise. Here, have a pear."

That evening, Sir Patrise died, and all the

knights and ladies of Camelot mourned—all except one. Sir Mador was delighted. This was even better than his original plan. He went to work. First he recovered the core of the pear. Then, for two nights, he shut himself up, reading books of old laws. On the third day, Sir Mador presented himself to the king and queen in the throne room.

"O King!" announced Sir Mador, "I bring you grave news. I have discovered that poor Sir Patrise's death was no accident. He was poisoned!"

"Poisoned?" exclaimed King Arthur. "But, who—?"

"The poison was in this pear," said Sir Mador, producing the core. "To discover the murderer, we must find who gave this to him to eat."

Queen Guinevere gasped. "But . . . but *I* gave Sir Patrise that pear!"

Sir Mador drew himself up and declared sternly, "Then Queen Guinevere, I charge you with murder! And because no judge in England

would dare rule against the queen, I claim my right as your accuser to call for a trial by combat!"

All the court buzzed with astonishment, and a murmur went up. "A trial by combat!"

Now, the trial by combat was an ancient custom in old England, almost forgotten in King Arthur's time. In this custom, when a person was accused of a crime, one knight took the side of the accused person and fought against the accuser to

decide the case. The idea was that the truth would always prevail, but what generally happened was that the side that had the strongest knight prevailed.

"But we haven't used the trial by combat in years," protested King Arthur.

"It is still the law of the land, is it not? I will prove Queen Guinevere's guilt with my own sword!"

As one, all of King Arthur's knights rose to their feet, each demanding the right to defend the queen, but Sir Mador held up his hand.

"Wait!" he said, pulling a roll of parchment from his tunic. "This is the law of the trial by combat, and it clearly states that when the accused person is a king or queen, then the defender must come from outside the court! None of the knights of the Round Table may take the queen's part! It is the law!"

The court lapsed into a stunned silence.

Sir Mador smiled evilly. "By law, you have one week to find a defender. If none appears, then the queen will be declared guilty, and you, O King, must order your own wife's execution." Turning, he strode triumphantly from the court.

❧ ❧

"Can't you just change the law?" wearily asked Sir Bedivere, one of King Arthur's advisors. The king and his council had spent the whole night searching through law books, but they could find no way around Sir Mador's demand.

"How can I claim to rule England with justice if I change the laws just to suit myself?" replied the king.

"I still don't understand why none of your own knights can fight for her," muttered Sir Gawain.

"Because if that were allowed," King Arthur explained, "then a king could do whatever he wanted. If anyone complained, he could just have his strongest knight call for a trial by combat and kill off his opposition—and it would all be legal. No, the law must be kept. We just have to find a champion to fight for the queen!"

"But where?" asked Sir Bedivere. "All the knights who love you are prohibited by law from defending her. The only knights who are allowed to take her part are recreant knights who hate you."

The king put his head in his hands. "I know," he said sadly. "Kay? What do you think?"

There was no answer. King Arthur raised his head and looked around the council room. Sir Kay was gone.

CHAPTER 9
The Oddly Made Knight

The day of the trial arrived, and although all the knights of the Round Table had scoured the country for a champion to fight for the queen, all had failed. As the law required, Queen Guinevere stood in an open field, bound by ropes, while her accuser, Sir Mador, waited in full armor for a challenger.

When no knight arrived, Sir Mador turned triumphantly to the king. "Does no one defend

Queen Guinevere of my charges? Then, by law, she must be declared guilty of murdering poor Sir Patrise and sentenced to death! You must pronounce sentence on your own queen now!" Sir Mador almost cackled with glee.

"Wait!" called a voice. The king and his court turned hopefully toward the sound.

From the woods at the edge of the field stepped the strangest-looking figure any had ever seen. It was a man, but he was wearing what looked like a garment of green twigs woven together and held in place with strips of bark. Leaves and branches bristled out like the quills of a large hedgehog. Over his face, the man wore a deerskin hood with holes cut in it for eyes, and from beneath the hood a bushy beard protruded. In the man's hand was a stout wooden staff.

"What . . . er, I mean, *who* are you?" asked King Arthur.

"I am a knight who has come to defend Queen

Guinevere," the man replied.

"You, a knight?" scoffed Sir Mador. "You look more like furniture!"

"You must forgive my armor," said the oddly made knight. "I didn't have any chain mail."

"And do you propose to fight me with a stick?"

"It was all that was handy. I've mislaid my sword, you see."

Sir Mador sneered at his twiggy opponent. "I find you insulting, oaf. I don't know what sort of low hovel you've crawled out of, but go back there at once before you annoy me."

"But I've come to fight you," said the oddly made knight.

"I don't lower myself to fight with peasants," said Sir Mador with a sneer.

"I spent hours putting this armor together. You think it was easy?"

"Go away, dolt, and do not meddle in the affairs of your betters!"

"You refuse to fight me?"

"I would throw you in a duck pond, but in that outfit you'd just float!"

"You refuse to fight me?" repeated the oddly made knight.

"Are you deaf as well as foolish?" snapped Sir Mador. "Yes! I refuse to fight you!"

The stranger turned to the king. "Sire, does not the law of the trial by combat state that if the accuser refuses to fight, then the accused must be set free?"

"So it does!" exclaimed King Arthur, leaping to his feet. "I hereby declare Queen Guinevere innocent! Release her at once!"

Stunned, Sir Mador stood still for a moment, then let out a bellow of rage. Drawing his sword, he charged the oddly made knight who had so neatly destroyed all his carefully made plans. The stranger sidestepped Sir Mador's flashing sword and, raising his wooden staff, struck Sir Mador in the head. He struck him very hard. The sound of the staff against Sir Mador's helmet was like the sound of an ax hitting a tree. Sir Mador's feet flew out from beneath him, and he landed on his back and did not move.

"And, Sire?" said the oddly made knight. "Does not the law say that a man who makes a false accusation must be banished from the land forever?"

"So it does," replied the king. "I hereby banish Sir Mador from England." Then he hesitated and added, "Starting as soon as he wakes up. I thank you, O knight, whoever you are."

The stranger removed the hood from his head. King Arthur stared for a long moment at the bushy-bearded face, then smiled. "Lancelot," he said.

At a great feast that night, Sir Kay, who had arrived at court shortly after Sir Lancelot, explained. "When Lancelot left last year, I followed him part of the way. I didn't want to lose my friend entirely. Then, when Sir Mador called for the trial by combat, I realized that there was only one knight who could defend the queen. After all, Lancelot had retired, so he wasn't from the king's court anymore."

"And so you went and found him," said the king.

"Not exactly, Sire," Sir Kay said. "If I'd found him, I would have lent him my own armor and sword. We're the same size, you know. Instead, what I found was an old hermit named Brastias who thought he knew where he was."

Then Sir Lancelot took up the tale. "Brastias had promised me that he would tell no one where I was, so instead of giving me away to Kay, he came himself and told me about the trial. I threw together some rough armor and left at once."

King Arthur smiled. "And we are glad that you did." Then his face grew solemn. "And now what? Will you leave us again?"

Slowly Sir Lancelot shook his head. "No, Sire. I have learned something about myself. I am supposed to be a knight. Not a knight who wins tournaments, not a knight who delights the ladies, not a knight in shining armor—just a knight who helps the helpless and defends the weak. With your permission, I would like to rejoin your Round Table."

King Arthur gave his permission, of course, and that was how Sir Lancelot returned to Camelot, where he remained the rest of his life, faithfully defending the defenseless, even when it interfered with his afternoon naps. He no longer competed in tournaments, and although he never again put on his armor of twigs, he adopted a new suit of armor that was so plain that as the years passed younger knights would shake their heads at his careless appearance. Sometimes they would even laughingly call him "Sir Lancelot the Shabby."

But to the storytellers—and, even more, to King Arthur, Queen Guinevere, and Sir Kay—he would always and forever be Sir Lancelot the Great.